CHILDREN'S THRIFT CLASSICS

Jewish Fairy Tales

GERALD FRIEDLANDER

Illustrated by Sheilah Beckett

DOVER PUBLICATIONS, INC.
Mineola, New York

DOVER CHILDREN'S THRIFT CLASSICS
EDITOR OF THIS VOLUME: SUSAN L. RATTINER

Copyright

Bibliographical Note

Jewish Fairy Tales, first published by Dover Publications, Inc., in 1997, is a new selection of 9 fairy tales from *The Jewish Fairy Book,* originally published by Frederick A. Stokes Company, New York, in 1920. The illustrations have been specially prepared for this edition.

Library of Congress Cataloging-in-Publication Data

Friedlander, Gerald, 1871–1923.
    [Jewish fairy book. Selections]
    Jewish fairy tales / Gerald Friedlander ; illustrated by Sheilah Beckett.
    p.   cm. — (Dover children's thrift classics)
    Contents: Chanina and the angels—The demon's marriage—The magic leaf—The princess and the beggar—Castle in the air—The snake's thanks—The goblin and the princess—David and the insects—Joseph, the Sabbath lover.
    Summary: Presents nine tales from various Jewish writings retold in a modern setting.
    ISBN 0-486-29861-2 (pbk.)
    1. Legends, Jewish. 2. Fairy tales. 3. Jews—Folklore. [1. Jews—Folklore. 2. Folklore. 3. Fairy tales.] I. Beckett, Sheilah, ill. II. Title. III. Series.
BM530.F742   1997
398.2'089'924—dc21
                                         97-14073
                                           CIP
                                         AC

Manufactured in the United States of America
Dover Publications, Inc., 31 East 2nd Street, Mineola, N.Y. 11501

Contents

Chanina and the Angels

WHILST THE Temple was still standing it was the custom of all the Jews to bring their sacrifices and gifts to Jerusalem. Rich and poor vied with one another in bringing offerings to the Holy House of God. Now there was a very poor man named Chanina who lived far away from the Holy City. In his own town he saw his fellow townsmen preparing themselves for their pilgrimage to Zion where the Temple was. Each one had an offering or present and he alone had nothing. He asked himself: "What can I find worthy of God's acceptance?"

He looked around in his humble home, but he could not find anything of value.

"All my neighbors," said he to himself, "will set out next week for Jerusalem taking their offerings with them and I, alas! will appear before the Lord empty-handed. This will not do, it must not be."

He then betook himself to the stone quarries near the town where he lived. He gazed around and saw a huge block of marble which had been placed on the rubbish heap, because its surface was too rough for polishing. He resolved to make its surface smooth, be the trouble never so great. From sunrise till sunset he worked. At last his patience and labor were rewarded. The surface of the stone became smooth and fit for polishing.

Chanina polished the marble from sunrise to sunset.

When this task was accomplished, Chanina rejoiced greatly.

"Now," he exclaimed, "this shall be my gift to God's Temple. The difficulty which now confronts me is, How am I to get this beautiful block to Jerusalem? I vow to give it to God's service and it must be taken to the Temple."

He returned to his town to look for carriers. He found a dozen men who could easily transport it. He asked them whether they would take the marble to the Holy City. They replied,—

"We will do what you want, if you pay us."

"Tell me, good friends, how much do you want?"

"One hundred golden coins."

"Where can I find such an immense sum of money? See," cried he, "this is all I possess; let me count. One, two, three, four, five pence. This is my total fortune. If you will trust me and should kind Providence help me to earn money, I will gladly pay you all you demand.

Now you are going to Jerusalem for the Festival and you might at the same time transport this marble, which I have vowed to give to the Sanctuary."

They laughed at him, as though he were joking, and went their way, leaving him alone. After a while he saw an old man coming along. When they met, the stranger greeted him and said,—

"What a fine block of marble! Do you know to whom it belongs?"

"I found it here some days ago cast on the rubbish heap. I have polished its surface and I have vowed to give it to the Temple."

"You have done well, my son. How will you have it removed to the Holy City?"

"That is just the difficulty which is troubling me at the present moment."

"Well, perhaps I can help you. I have five servants yonder. If you will lend a hand, I think we can transport it."

"Most gladly will I do as you say, and in addition I will pay you five pence, all I possess at present."

"So be it."

At that moment five tall men came forward and at once placed their hands on the marble. As in a blinding storm they rushed along, carried by the huge block, and before many seconds had passed Chanina found himself beside the marble in the Temple Court. He rubbed his eyes, for he thought that he was dreaming, but when he saw the priests and the Levites coming towards him he knew that he was wide awake.

"The Lord be with thee, O Chanina," they cried.

"May the Lord bless you!" he answered.

He then turned round to look for the old man and his five men, but they had vanished. He wanted to give them the five pence which he had promised to pay. He

Chanina asked the priest to give the money to the poor.

then asked the priests to accept the marble as his gift for the coming festival, and he also handed to them the five pence, asking them to distribute the money to the poor. With great joy in his heart he thanked God for the miracle which had befallen him. He said to himself,—

"I believe the old man was Elijah the prophet, and the five men with him were ministering angels. The wonders of the Lord never cease."

Chanina felt his coat pressing rather heavily on his shoulders. He put his hands into his pockets, and he was amazed to find them full of golden coins. He rejoiced at this fresh token of Heaven's favor, and when he returned home he had sufficient money to spend his days in comfort.

The Demon's Marriage

LONG, LONG ago, in quite the olden time, there lived a King who had an only daughter. The monarch was very wealthy and he was exceedingly proud of being so rich. To be sure, he had much more money than he deserved to have. He thought more about money than about anything else. He was also haughty because he wore a crown. He listened to silly people who told him that his blood was blue, because he was a King. "Like father, like child," says an old proverb, and the Princess was also very proud. She loved money, and thought herself better than everybody else.

When a poor noble Prince came to woo her, she would refuse to listen to his heart's cry; telling him that his rank was not good enough, or that his money was far too little for her ideas. In fact, she thought that money was the only thing worth having in life. Her father, instead of rebuking her and correcting her, encouraged her to look for rank and wealth as the first qualifications in any suitor. In fact, he used to say that he would never allow her to marry any one unless he happened to be a Prince who had as much money as he had.

Many suitors came to win her hand, but she rejected them. Some of these men were noble and good men; their only fault was their poverty. One day when she

5

was celebrating her twenty-third birthday her father said to her,—

"I do wish, dear daughter, that Princes who are beggars would keep away from our court."

"To be sure, dear father, I quite agree. I have no patience with poor people who think of marrying me for the sake of my wealth."

A handsome young fellow appeared in the palace, dressed in silk and velvet.

Not long after this conversation there appeared in the courtyard of the palace a handsome young fellow dressed like a Prince in silk and velvet. His sword was of gold, and he had diamonds in the buckles of his shoes. He knocked at the palace door and when it was opened he asked to see the King. He was admitted and conducted at once to the royal presence. He advanced towards the throne whereon the King sat, and, after bowing in a very stately fashion, exclaimed,—

"May your gracious Majesty live long and live well! I am a Prince with very blue blood; my pedigree is unparalleled, I can assure you. I have come to ask your Majesty's permission to woo your lovely daughter. I am longing to see her, for I hear that she is the most beautiful Princess in all the world. The fame of her beauty has reached my father's realm, and I now ask you to allow me to see her."

"Well, noble Prince, I think I can allow you to see her. Like all wise Princesses, she has made up her mind to be uninfluenced in her love affairs. I cannot help you. What I will do, however, is to second your efforts, if my daughter seems favorably disposed towards you."

He then ordered his chamberlain to request the Princess to come to the throne-room.

"Tell her royal highness," he added, "that a most noble Prince is being received in audience and desires to make her royal highness' acquaintance."

After a few minutes' interval, the Princess entered the throne-room and sat on a chair of state beside her father. She looked very beautiful and her court jewels added to her adornment.

"Permit me to greet your royal highness," said the visitor, "and will you favor me by accepting this small gift which I have brought from my royal father."

He then gave her a gold casket full of brilliants and pearls. There were rings and bracelets set with glistening diamonds and rubies. She gazed for some time at the wonderful sight, and when she had feasted her eyes sufficiently she cried aloud,—

"Look, father dear! See what a wonderful gift this charming Prince has brought me. Never before did I

"Look at the wonderful gift this charming Prince has brought me!"

receive such a lovely present. I cannot find words to thank the Prince."

"Truly wonderful and right royal is the gift," said the King, and turning to his daughter he said: "Now leave us."

"Now may I speak?" said the Prince with a smile on his face. "I have come to win the hand and heart of your lovely daughter. I am indeed so much in love with her that I venture to ask you to consent to my endeavor to win her love. I know you will not allow her to wed a poor Prince. I feel sure that I can satisfy you that I am not only as wealthy as your Majesty, but I can claim to possess more money than can be found in your kingdom. I am, of course, of noble descent as I have already mentioned. My father rules a great kingdom and I am the heir-apparent."

"By all appearances," observed the King, "your royal highness seems to be a very wealthy and noble Prince. I must confess that I have been agreeably surprised by your kindness in giving my daughter such a magnificent present."

"Oh, your Majesty!" said the Prince, "pray do not mention this again. It was a mere bagatelle compared with the jewels I have with me here in my apartments. If your Majesty will honor me by accompanying me to my rooms I will be able to show your Majesty a small portion of my wealth. I do not like to boast, but I must tell you that I have with me antique and precious gems of greater value than all the crown jewels of your Majesty. Such things as I possess your Majesty has never seen. All this is as nothing compared with the wealth in my castles and palace at home. All this fortune awaits my future wife. I hope it will be your daughter. Have I your consent?"

"What is the name of your father's kingdom, and what is your own name?"

"I am called Prince Daring and my father's realm is called the Kingdom of Delight; it is situated far away beyond the hills, across the sea. Probably in such a small kingdom as this your Majesty has never heard of this realm. Do not your subjects say, 'The proof of the pudding is in the eating'? Here I am, at all events, and you can judge what sort of Prince I am. Your own eyes shall have abundant proof as to my enormous wealth. I imagine your experience tells you that you can recognize in me the exterior of a Prince the like of whom you have rarely seen at your court. Kindly tell me now whether I am acceptable to your Majesty as a future son-in-law."

"I will give my decision when I have seen your treasures."

"Will your Majesty accompany me now to my rooms?"

"We will go at once."

The King went with the Prince to his lodging, which was in one of the best hotels in the city. The King was astounded to see in one of the rooms more gold, silver, jewels, and precious material than he had ever seen in all his life.

"Well, I never," observed the King, "expected to see such wealth and treasure; you must be a hundred times richer than I am. Of course you have my consent to wed my sweet daughter. I am sure you will make a very good son-in-law."

They then returned to the palace. The King sent for the Princess and told her that he quite approved of the Prince as her future husband. The Princess with a blush on her face said,—

"I am quite happy to be the bride of such a noble Prince whose wealth will enable us to be happy and to enjoy life in a manner becoming our rank."

The Prince placed a diamond ring on her finger, and kissed her.

"Of that there can be no doubt," said the King.

"Yes, you shall have as much money as you want, sweet Princess," said the Prince.

"I shall realize my dream of having heaps and heaps of money, amusement will make me so happy," said the Princess with joy in her eyes.

The Prince then placed a lovely diamond engagement ring on the finger of the Princess, saying: "With this ring do I betroth thee unto me." He then kissed her. But she seemed to be chilled by his cold lips and she trembled for a second. Her father wished her joy and kissed her. The King summoned his courtiers and told of his daughter's engagement. The happy bridal couple received the congratulations of the entire court. Heralds were sent to all parts of the kingdom to proclaim the good news. The people rejoiced when they heard that the Princess had at last found a husband.

Elaborate preparations for the royal wedding were at once taken in hand. The marriage was fixed to take place in a week's time. All the nobles and the rich merchants were invited to witness the function and to attend the State ball which was to follow the happy event. The banquet after the marriage ceremony was truly royal. The best of everything was provided in abundance. The choicest wines were taken from the royal cellars. The King determined to make an effort in order to impress his rich son-in-law. He spared no expense to provide a magnificent feast, and he succeeded so well that all his guests were surprised and delighted.

After the first week of their married life, the Prince came to his father-in-law and said,—

"Beloved father of my wife! I crave your Majesty's permission to return to my own land and home with my dear wife. I promised my good father that I should not be

absent from his court for more than twenty days. I have
spent fourteen days here as your guest and I took three
days to come here and I need three days for the return
journey. My time is now up. I dare not disappoint the
King my father lest he be angry with me and your daughter. It would never do for my sweet wife to meet her
father-in-law in one of his dreadful tempers. He is liable
to fits of wicked temper, and if I am not greatly mistaken
most monarchs are subject to the same trouble."

"Yes, yes," cried the King somewhat testily. "I am also
in a temper occasionally and I shall soon fly into a very
bad one if you talk about going away so suddenly. This
unexpected news has quite upset me—dear me! This is
too bad. Just stay one more day to please me. If you
hurry away so suddenly the courtiers will think that we
have had a quarrel or that something is wrong."

"Your Majesty surely knows by now that I would
most gladly do anything to give you pleasure, but I cannot disobey my father. I must therefore say 'Good-by'
now, and I once again thank you for giving me your
beautiful and sweet daughter. I will take every care of
her and you will hear from us in due course."

The King saw that the Prince was determined to
depart. He therefore gave his consent with the best
grace he could command. He gave orders for a large
retinue to accompany the Princess and her husband.
He told his daughter that she might take with her his
court harpist and retain him as one of her attendants in
her new home. Prior to his departure the Prince gave
beautiful presents to all the court officials and also a
large box of jewels to the King. At last the bride and
bridegroom left the palace. The King stood on the bal-
cony and waved his hand to his daughter. Every mark
of honor was naturally shown to the Prince and

Princess. Away the cortège went, many of the followers being afoot, the rest on horseback.

On the third day after their departure they saw in the distance a large and beautiful city. The Prince then turned to all who had followed him and said,—

"Yonder is the capital of my father's kingdom. I now wish to bid you all farewell. Return to your homes, as I do not wish to trouble you to accompany me any longer. I thank you for your courtesy in coming thus far. I appreciate your attention very much indeed."

The retinue heard these words in great surprise. They begged him to allow them to accompany him a little further.

"If we may not," said they, "come as far as the castle, let us at all events see you and our dear Princess enter the city gates. We will then return home."

"You will return now or not at all," cried the Prince with flashing eyes. "I almost feel inclined to enjoy the pleasure of doing a little evil to all of you. You are, one and all, in my power. You think that I am a Prince. I am nothing of the kind. You imagine that I am a human being. You are mightily mistaken."

"What are you then?" they cried in dismay.

"I am a demon in human shape. Were it not for the fact that you have been very courteous to me and the Princess my wife, I would not suffer you to return at all. I should keep you here in my kingdom as prisoners and slaves. I went to your lord the King to punish him for his abominable pride. He loves money more than anything else. Virtue, character and true nobility do not count in his eyes. He prefers appearances to reality— and for once in his life he has got his preference. Your King asked me my name: go and tell him that I am the son of Satan. You will not easily forget it once you have heard it. I know that my personality usually makes a great impression. I think your King and master will remember me all the days of his life. In giving the Princess to me he thought the lines of her life were being laid in pleasant places. But pleasant places are not to be bought with money. It is not all gold that glitters. The love of money is a terrible spell that casts misfortune and unhappiness upon all those who love it above all things. When people are ready to sell body and soul for gold and silver there is no hope for them. Your King has sold his daughter to the Devil and there is no hope for either of them."

When the Princess heard these terrible words she screamed in fright and fell to the earth in a dead faint. She was quickly raised up from the ground by the harpist, who was so sweet and gentle in all his ways. He led her to a tuft of grass where she could rest herself. The retainers stood still as though they were bewitched. At last one of them turned to the disguised demon and said,—

"What proof can you give us that what you say is the truth?"

"Proof, indeed!" cried he. "See!" He touched the ground with his golden sword and lo! a column of fire and smoke arose from the earth. "I will give you further proof," he added. "I now command all the jewels and gifts which I gave to the King and the officials on the day of my departure to change into tinsel and dross. You will see that this has happened when you reach the palace. Now tell me when will that be if you return at once?"

"Why, in three days, of course," said they. "Is to-day not the third day since we left the King?"

"Yes, that is correct, but you will not be able to reach your homes in three days. When I am with you the way

He touched the ground with his golden sword
and a column of fire arose from the earth.

is soon covered. As soon as you leave me it will take you three weeks to cover the same ground which took me but three days. If this should prove to be true, you need have no hesitation in telling your master all that you have seen and all that I have spoken. Now, good folk, begone! I am tired of talking and I want to take my wife to the castle without any further delay. Farewell."

The retainers had barely heard the last word when they saw the Prince and Princess, followed by the harpist, leaving them. They therefore determined to get back home as quickly as possible. They were terribly afraid and they were exceedingly glad to escape from the demon. As he had foretold they spent three weeks on their return journey.

When at last they reached their homes they heard that the King was in the greatest distress. He declared that he had been swindled. To his courtiers he said,—

"See! this box of jewels which my son-in-law gave me is not now worth a penny. It is full of imitation rubbish, tinsel not fit to be seen in my palace."

When he heard the tale of the retainers he swooned and never regained consciousness. The news that his only daughter had married a demon was too much for him. His pride was struck low. He lingered on for two days and then he died, much to the regret of his servants.

Meanwhile the demon Prince and his beautiful young bride had reached the castle where they were to live. The town in which the castle stood was inhabited by gnomes and fairies, the subjects of King Satan. Of course there were no human beings in the town except the unfortunate Princess and her trusty harpist. The Princess had longed to ask her husband to suffer her to return to her father when he had dismissed the retinue, but she was afraid that not only would he refuse her request but that probably he would kill her on the spot. She now knew that her foolish pride had met with its just punishment. She submitted to her awful fate with a resignation born of despair. Her only solace was the company of the talented harpist, whose sweet music enchanted her and made her forget her terrible doom. Her demon husband also professed to admire the skill of the musician, saying,—

"I am a great lover of good music, and I must confess that I consider your harpist to be a real artist. I am glad you brought him with you."

Three years passed, and one day the Prince came to his wife when she was listening to the strains of the harp. He listened for awhile, and then standing up cried aloud,—

"Enough! Now, dear wife, your time to depart hence has come."

"What do you mean?" she cried with terror in her eyes.

"You must come away from this home."

"Whither must I go?"

"You must go to Hell," said he with a horrible grin on his handsome face.

The unfortunate Princess knew that to resist would be madness. She arose and said, "I am ready, lead on." Her husband went in front of her and she followed with a heavy heart. She recalled her past life and regretted her folly in refusing to listen to the many good men who

Her husband went in front of her
and she followed with a heavy heart.

had desired to win her hand. "I was blind," she murmured, "not to see the real and true men. I am now reaping the harvest of my sin. I rejected the genuine and now I have the sham."

At last they came to the grim portals of Hell, which are never closed. He handed her over to the custody of the sleepless guardians who are ever ready to receive their unhappy victims.

"Farewell, sweet wife! You are going to the fiery furnace where not only gold and silver are tried but where hearts and souls are also tested and judged. I am sorry I cannot accompany you," he added in a harsh voice that seemed to whip her soul at every word, "but I can tell you that you will meet with strict justice. Listen, and let me prepare you for your fate. You will be in a little world where everything you touch will turn into gold. You will like that, for you love gold. The bread you would eat will become gold as soon as you put it to your mouth. The water you take to quench your thirst will change into molten gold directly you put your goblet to your lips. The fruit you grasp will become golden in your hand. Gold and gold will be your punishment for all eternity. Farewell!"

She passed within and he turned his back and left the last abode of the hopeless.

Her faithful harpist had accompanied her till she came to the portals of Hell. He then withdrew a step or two. He gazed in front of him, curious to know what Hell looked like.

"Whom do I see yonder?" he exclaimed in surprise. "Well, I am shocked to see my old friend Nathan the harpist with his harp in this terrible place. Hullo! old Nathan, what are you doing here?"

"As you see, I am playing my harp in Hell. Good friend, beware! Do not advance a step nearer, do not fol-

low the beautiful lady who has just been admitted. If
you do you will be in Hell, and once here there is no
return. I will henceforth look after her and play to her
whenever I am permitted to do so."

"Thanks very much for your good advice, which I
shall be most careful to follow. Now be good enough to
tell me, dear friend, how is it that although you are in
Hell you are not burning with Hell's fire?"

"I will gladly tell you the reason why I am not burning. When I came here I was asked by the angels of
mercy, justice and righteousness, whether I could
remember having done any act of justice or deed of
love or work of righteousness. After much thought I
could only recall one good deed in my life."

"I am playing my harp in Hell.
Do not advance a step nearer—there is no return."

"What was that?"

"Don't be in such a hurry. We are very patient here and you must give me time to tell you. My good deed was the following. I was always glad to play my harp free of charge at the weddings of the poor in order that they also might for once in their wretched lives have a happy time and enjoy their wedding festivity by means of my harp's sweet strains. This saved me and my harp from Hell's fire."

"Thanks awfully for this piece of valuable information. I shall take a leaf out of your book. Your example shall find in me an excellent follower. Tell me, good Nathan, do you really think I shall escape Hell's fire if I do as you did? Stay—I will do more. I will also give half of all my earnings to the poor. I receive good pay when I play in the houses of the rich and I can well afford to give half away. I will always be ready to play free of charge at the weddings of the poor. I will also try every day to make some one happy, for we know that the strains of the harp drive away grief and cares."

"Do all that and you will never be in Hell at all."

"Good! Now tell me, dear Nathan, how am I to find my way home: which road must I take?"

"Keep to the right and go straight forward. I am very sorry I am unable to leave this dreary place. I should be so happy to accompany you on your return to the lovely world. But it cannot be."

"Many thanks for directing me. You can do me just one more favor."

"Well, what do you want?"

"Give me some sign or token to prove that I have spoken to you. If, by the grace of God, I return to my home, I shall, of course, tell my friends of all that I have seen and heard. When I say that I saw my good friend Nathan in Hell my audience will laugh at me and in derision they will exclaim: 'O yes! what a delightful fairy tale you are telling.' When I reply that it is not a fairy tale but the sober truth they will all cry out in chorus, 'Prove it.' Now just help me to prove my tale."

"Very well. Stretch out the little finger of your left hand and reach over until it is about half-an-inch in here. I will then come as near as I can and touch it. You will immediately have all the proof you need."

"Stretch out the little finger of your left hand and you will have all the proof you need."

"I am ready. Here we are touching one another. . . . Stop it, please, you are burning my finger. It is not only burning, it is shining with a blue light and smells of sulphur. Enough! I have proof, much more than I ever wished to have! Can't you help me to get rid of the burning pain and the shining effect? I don't like it at all."

"No, no, be satisfied. It is only the tip of your finger and not your whole body that is on fire. Now go the way I pointed out, and all will be well. Farewell, and don't come back."

"Farewell."

Nathan saw his friend with his harp under his arm beginning his return journey. On and on he went, and after wandering many days in strange lands, crossing hills and dales, fields and deserts, he came at last to his own city. How glad he was to reach his home! All who saw him were astonished to see his burning and shining finger. The harpist kept his word and played for the poor free of charge. He gave away in charity half of his earnings. The more he played on his harp the cooler grew his finger. At last it became quite normal, while the music of his harp became sweeter and sweeter till it one day charmed the old harpist into the sweetest sleep of his long and hard life. He still sleeps on, hearing the harmonies of love and charity.

The Magic Leaf

ONCE UPON a time there lived on the banks of the Euphrates in Babylon a holy man who spent his days and nights in the performance of religious rites and in meditation. He determined to go to the Holy Land in order to end his days in Jerusalem, where the Temple of God stood. On and on he went and at sundown he felt very tired, and sat down to rest his weary feet. He would have been glad to fall asleep but was unable to do so owing to the loud twittering of the birds overhead. He sat up watching. He saw two of the birds quarreling, while the others went on chirping for all they were worth. At last one of the two birds that were quarreling killed the other, whereupon all the rest took to flight. The holy man sat still, for he was curious to learn what would happen.

He did not have to wait very long before he saw a large bird flying towards him. The bird passed him and came near to its dead brother. In its little beak it held a small green leaf which it placed on the head of the dead bird. Immediately the leaf touched it, a wonderful miracle happened. It was re-animated and stood upon its feet. It shook its pretty feathers, flapped its wings and flew off.

The man was astounded at what he had seen. He sprang up, saying to himself,—

23

*He tucked the leaf into his turban,
and spent the night beneath a tree.*

"I must get that magic leaf, it will enable me to quicken all the dead in the Holy Land when I arrive there. This is truly a most extraordinary slice of luck to find such a priceless treasure. I suppose this leaf comes from the tree of life in the Garden of Eden. Had I not witnessed the miracle I should never have believed it possible. This leaf is worth untold gold and will bring me good fortune and happiness."

He picked up the leaf and put it away carefully in the fold of his turban. He resolved to spend the night beneath a tree near by, as no houses were visible. Next day he awoke very early. The sun rose, scattering with his powerful beams the morning mists.

He pursued his journey after he had said his morning prayers. He had not walked many hours when he came to a farm. He was about to enter in order to ask for food, when he saw just outside the doorway a dead fox. He went up to it and said to himself,—

"Now I will get out the magic leaf and see if it will re-animate this dead fox. I like to experiment with this most wonderful leaf."

He took off his turban and took out the precious leaf, which he put on the head of the fox. No sooner had the leaf touched the fox, than the latter jumped up and ran away as quickly as his legs could carry him.

"This is marvelous," he exclaimed, while picking up the leaf, which he replaced in the fold of his turban.

He then knocked at the door of the farm-house and was admitted. He asked for a little food which was readily given him by the owner, an old farmer.

"Did you know there was a dead fox outside your door?" he asked the farmer.

The latter replied, "Of course I did, for I killed him yesterday."

The Visitor: "The fox is not there now."

Farmer: "Where is he?"

Visitor: "He ran away just before I knocked at your door."

Farmer: "That is impossible."

Visitor: "Go and look. You will not see the fox."

Farmer: "Come with me and let us look together." They went to the door, and sure enough the fox was not to be seen.

Visitor: "I brought the dead fox back to life. I am a holy man and I can revive the dead."

Farmer: "You are a foolish chatterbox. If what you say be true, take my advice and do not meddle with the mysteries of life and death. God alone will quicken the dead. Now, farewell."

The farmer went into his house and shut the door. Whereupon the holy man went on his way, thinking that

The lion sprang upon the holy man and devoured him.

God had given him such a wonderful treasure because he had lived such a holy life.

"The old farmer does not understand the good fortune which has befallen me," he muttered.

He had not proceeded very far when he saw a dead lion in the road. He thought of testing once more the efficacy of the wonderful leaf.

"This shall be my last experiment," he said, as he took off his turban.

He then took out the magic leaf and placed it on the head of the lion. This was no sooner done than the lion arose and growled with delight at seeing a fine meal in front of him in the shape of the holy man. The next instant, as the holy man began to regret his extreme folly in restoring the dead lion to life, the latter sprang upon him and devoured him. The lion also ate the magic leaf. With this disaster the possibility of reviving the dead passed away and mortals must now wait patiently for the quickening of the dead till the great day of the resurrection comes.

The Princess and the Beggar

NOW KING SOLOMON had a daughter, who was the most beautiful princess in the world. On her fifteenth birthday her wise father made up his mind to look at the stars in the heavens and to read therein the fate of his beloved child. That night he gazed at the constellations in the sky and discovered that the lovely princess was destined to become the wife of a beggar whose poverty was to be greater than that of any one in his kingdom. He also read in the stars that his daughter and her future husband would be blessed with children. King Solomon turned his eyes from the heavens in shame and anger. This outlook for his daughter's future happiness was not at all to his liking. "I wish I had not been so inquisitive," said he to himself. "Why did I try to read the future? Now I know what is her destiny I am wretched and unhappy. I will take steps to prevent such an unfortunate marriage. It's not fair that marriages should be arranged in heaven."

That same night he went to his study and rubbed his magic ring on which the Holy Name of God was engraved. Before him stood Ashmodai, King of the Genii. "Gracious Master, command and I will obey thy will."

"Listen then, Ashmodai. Near the sea-coast opposite

Joppa is a small rock in the sea. I wish to have a very lofty tower built on this rock. The base of the tower must cover the entire surface of the rock except where the steps lead to the entrance."

"Before sundown to-morrow, O son of David! thy wish shall be fulfilled." The next moment the demon had vanished.

On the next day the King sent for the beautiful princess and told her that she would in three days' time go with him to one of his castles near the sea and reside there for some time. "Thy will is my pleasure, O dearest of fathers," said the princess when she heard her father's wish. At the appointed time the King and the princess with a retinue of seventy servants set out for the port of Joppa. When they arrived there they embarked on the King's ship and sailed to the rocky shore where the tower stood. The rooms were furnished in a most princely manner. There was everything that one could wish for. Of course there was also a sufficient store of food in the tower for all the needs of the princess and her attendants. The King told the attendants that they were to watch by day and night and see to it that no stranger set foot within the tower. "As soon as the princess and you are all in the tower I will have the only door, which is at the entrance, removed and replaced by brickwork. You are to prevent any communication whatsoever reaching her. If you disobey, your lives will be forfeit." The King kissed his daughter and warned her not to try to escape. "In good time I will fetch thee and then thou shalt live in my palace on Mount Lebanon. Now farewell." She promised her father to obey and waved her hand as she saw him embark on the royal ship. "Good-by," she cried with a sad voice, standing on the roof. She did not quite like the idea of being shut up in the lonely tower.

*The servants follow the King's orders
to brick up the doorway of the tower.*

While the King was embarking, his servants were removing the door of the tower and bricking up the doorway. It was now impossible for any one to enter or leave and the only means of exit was through a skylight on the roof.

On his journey home King Solomon smiled and said to himself: "I will now see if my plan will be a success. I think I shall for once in a while have my own way. After all this lovely girl is my child and I can surely arrange her marriage as I like. I am not satisfied with the choice of the bridegroom made by the stars. A beggar should marry the daughter of a beggar but not the daughter of a king. I shall wait and see. Whatever happens will, I hope, be for the best."

About three years later it happened that on a certain day a beggar left his home in Acco, a seaport north of Mount Carmel. He could not find even a crust of dry bread in his town and he determined to seek his fortune whithersoever his Heavenly Father might direct his steps. He had spent all his time since childhood in studying the Holy Law. His beggarly clothes were all in tatters. On and on he went, hungry and thirsty. He had no idea where he would be able to find a night's lodging. "Ah!" said he to himself, "what a funny world we are in. Rich and poor, wise and foolish, happy and unhappy people live according to the will of God. He it is who bringeth low and raiseth up, who maketh poor and maketh rich. What is my fate? God alone knows." On and on he tramped. The sun was beginning to set and the air grew cold. He then saw something that attracted his attention. It was in a field just off the highway. He went to see what it was. He found that it was the hide of an ox. "This is lucky," cried he in delight; "God has now provided me with a night's lodging. I will roll myself in this skin and escape the cold wind. I will sleep as happily as though I were in a warm cozy bed." He said his night prayers and asked God to send his good angels to watch around him and to take charge over him. In a minute he was tightly rolled up in the skin and in the twinkling of an eye he slept the sweet sleep of the weary.

The moon was shining brightly. A mountain eagle flew near by and seeing the skin rolled up mistook it for the dead body of an ox. He pounced upon it and seized it with his talons and bore it high up in the air. On and on he flew, across hill and dale, over river and sea, till he reached the tower on the rock in the sea near Joppa. He dropped the heavy hide on the roof of the tower at the break of day. The eagle flew away to his nest on the hills, intending to return later in the day with his family and to dine off the flesh of the ox which he thought was beneath the hide.

No sooner had the eagle dropped his burden than the beggar awoke and held his breath, for he knew neither where he was nor what had befallen him. Hearing the flapping of the eagle in his flight to his nest, the poor man ventured to get out of the hide to see where he was. He was more than amazed to find himself on the roof of the huge tower surrounded by the sea. He said to himself: "How shall I ever escape from this lonely place? Hark! Who's that opening the sky-light? See, here's a strange sight, the like of which I have never

He was amazed to find himself on the roof
of the tower surrounded by the sea.

seen. Is it a fairy yonder? Who has ever seen such a lovely face, such eyes as blue as the sky, such hair like gold in the sunshine? It must be a fairy princess or I am still dreaming. Look, she is coming nearer and nearer to me. She is going to speak—"

"I am in the habit of taking a little exercise out here every morning before breakfast. Little did I ever expect to see a stranger here. Please excuse the liberty I take in speaking first, but this is my home. I like to know the names of all who come here. Now tell me, please, who art thou and how didst thou get here?"

"Gracious lady! I am a Jew, a student of the Holy Law of Israel. My home is in Acco, in the land ruled by the wisest of kings, Solomon. My father and mother are no longer on this earth. I am very poor and I left home yesterday to seek my bread whithersoever God might lead me. After sunset I went to sleep in a field, wrapping myself in the hide of an ox. I was so happy in my sleep, dreaming sweet dreams. All of a sudden I awoke by falling heavily on this roof. When I opened the hide and came out I saw a huge eagle flying over the sea. I am sure that this bird brought me here. Now I pray thee, good lady, forgive me for being here uninvited. Pray let me descend and depart."

"That is impossible."

"Why?"

"There is no door to this tower."

"Am I bewitched?"

"I do not think so."

"Art thou a fairy?"

"Of course not."

"Why is there no door to the tower?"

"So that no one shall enter or depart. And even if there was a door, escape is impossible. We are on a rock in the middle of the sea. Boatmen are not allowed to come near to the tower unless it be by the King's order."

"Do not look at me. I am so ashamed of my rags."

"That is easily put right. Come with me and I will show thee a nice room where new clothes are at thy disposal. There thou wilt also be able to have a good wash and make thyself comfortable. Then we will have breakfast together."

"This is all too lovely. Is it all true? Am I still dreaming?"

"Not at all."

"I am most grateful for all thy kindness. I shall be most happy to be thy guest for the present."

The princess led the beggar to the room and left him at the door, after telling where he was to find her for breakfast. When he had washed and changed his clothes he came to the princess. He was the most handsome man she had ever seen. There and then she fell in love with him. She asked him whether he would like to marry her. He at once consented. In his great joy he said to her: "I will now write out our marriage contract."

She gave him parchment and a quill, saying, "I am very sorry to tell thee that I cannot find any ink."

"That matters not. I can supply a good substitute."

"What will it be?"

"See, I will just open this little vein in my arm and with a few drops of blood I will write the deed."

He did so. Then taking her right hand he slipped on her forefinger a golden ring which his dying mother had given him and which he had on his little finger. "Behold," he cried, "with this ring do I betroth thee unto me and marry thee according to the Law of Moses and Israel, God and His angels Michael and Gabriel being our witnesses."

In time they had a sweet little daughter. News of this unexpected event was duly reported by Ashmodai to King Solomon. He at once set out to visit the princess. When he reached the rock on which the tower stood, he carefully examined the brickwork which had replaced the doorway. It had not been touched. The King now ordered his servants to remove the bricks and to replace the door. He then entered the tower. All the attendants were summoned to meet King Solomon. They were in mortal dread, fearing that their lord would punish them with death on account of what had happened. When the King saw them he said:

"Do ye know anything about the marriage of the princess? Were ye present at the ceremony?"

"No, your gracious Majesty."

"I will go and ask the princess to tell me the truth, wait ye here till I return."

The King went to the room of the princess and after greeting her he asked her:

"Is it true that thou art married?"

"Of course, dearest father."

"Who is thy husband?"

"A noble Jew. God sent him to me. He is the most handsome man in the kingdom. I fell in love with him at first sight. I asked him to have me for his wife. He agreed most kindly and I am glad he was good enough to fulfill my wish. I hope, father dear, that thou art come to bless our darling baby, my husband and me. My husband is a great scholar. He knows the Holy Law by heart. He is a noble and good man."

"I can see, my child, that thou dost love him."

"That indeed I do."

"Call him and let us see one another."

The princess went to fetch him. When he saw the King, he fell on his face to the ground and cried:

"Tell me all about thy family and thy history."

"Long live King Solomon!"

"I understand from my daughter here that thou art her husband."

"Even as thou sayest, O lord King."

"Hast thou a marriage contract?"

"Here it is."

"Tell me all about thy family and thy history."

When he had told the King all that he desired to know, Solomon embraced him and blessed him. He saw that this poor youth was the very man destined to be his daughter's husband. After all, marriages are made in Heaven. Solomon rejoiced when he found his son-in-law to be a learned and good man, fit to be married to the most beautiful princess in the whole world. They lived very happily all the days of their life, leaving several sons and daughters to mourn their loss when they slept into death in a ripe old age.

The Castle in the Air

L ONG, LONG ago there lived two famous kings. One
was Pharaoh, king of Egypt. The other was
Sennacherib, king of Assyria. Pharaoh was a very war-
like ruler. He had an enormous army. His soldiers were
very brave and most skillful with their bows and battle-
axes. Their King delighted to see them daily on parade
in the sandy desert near the royal palace. He watched
them in summer and in winter. His object in having his
fine men constantly drilled was to have them ready for
battle, which he would have gladly welcomed should
occasion arise to wage war. He often wished, as he rode
home to his palace after drill, that he had a palace or
castle in the desert. But he knew that the sand of the
desert would never do for a foundation and therefore it
was useless to build his residence there.

One day a rumor reached him that the King of
Assyria had caused his wise Minister of State, named
Achikar, to be killed. Pharaoh had always been afraid of
having a quarrel with this man, who knew so well how
to advise his master King Sennacherib. Now that he
was supposed to be dead there was nothing to fear.
Therefore Pharaoh wrote a very rude letter to the king
of Assyria as follows: "Health be to thee. It is good for
kings to pay tribute to those who are wiser and

stronger than they are. Thou must either pay tribute to
me or I must give thee tribute. Be it known to thee that
I desire to have a castle built in the air over the desert
of Egypt. I know that it is not a very easy thing to have
a castle between heaven and earth. It is very good for
kings to learn how to do difficult tasks. I therefore order
thee to send me within six months a clever man who is
a skilled architect, that is to say, a man who can draw
the plans of the castle and guide the workmen. He must
also bring with him builders for the work. When thou
hast sent me such men I will collect and send thee the
taxes of Egypt for three years. If, however, thou
shouldst neglect this my request and fail to send me
such men of whom I have written above, then shalt
thou collect and send me as tribute the taxes of Assyria
for three years. Failing this, I will gather my mighty
army and come to fight thee. I will lay waste thy land
and take away thy kingdom. From thy overlord,
Pharaoh, King of Egypt."

As soon as this letter reached Sennacherib, he read it
and handed it to his Ministers of State. They advised
him to summon all his nobles and to ask their advice,
saying, "What shall we do?" He followed this plan.
When the nobles had heard the letter read, they held
their peace. Their silence distressed Sennacherib, who
did not know what was to be done. He then called
together all the old and learned men, including the star-
gazers and magicians. As soon as they were all seated
in the royal council room, the King told them what the
King of Egypt had dared to write. "How shall I act, what
advice do ye give?"

"O Lord, great King!" said one of the star-gazers,
"know that there is none in thy kingdom who could deal
with King Pharaoh except the wise Achikar, the royal
secretary. Alas! he was put to death at thy command.

Why ask us to advise thee? Who is able to build a castle in the air between heaven and earth? We cannot help thee."

Now as a matter of fact it was unknown to the King Sennacherib that Achikar was not dead at all. He had

Sennacherib read the letter and handed it to his Ministers of State.

been condemned to death on a false charge of betraying his king and country. On the day when he was supposed to suffer death, he had recognized in the public executioner a friend, whose life he had once saved. In return the kind-hearted friend spared his life and a condemned criminal took Achikar's place at the public execution.

When King Sennacherib found that there was no one in his kingdom to help him, he began to lament over Achikar's death. In the hearing of all his courtiers he said: "Alas for thee, noble and wise Achikar! How well didst thou manage the affairs of our kingdom! All the secrets and thoughts of men didst thou know. Woe is me for thee! how did I destroy thee. I listened to the tittle-tattle of evil men and in consequence thou art no more. Ah! who can give thee to me just for once, or bring me word that thou art alive? I would give him half of my kingdom. Moreover, I would also give him thy weight in gold."

With tears in his sad eyes the King sat on his throne of gold after he had spoken these words. Then one of the courtiers present came near to the king and said: "O king! live forever. I was the public executioner when Achikar was sentenced to death. Now command thy servants to cut off my head."

"Why should I do this?"

"O my lord! every one that doeth not the order of the king is worthy of death."

"That is right. What hast thou failed to do?"

"I have disobeyed the king's command."

"When and how?"

"Thou didst command me to put Achikar to death. I knew that one day thou wouldst repent thee concerning him. I was also aware that he had been very greatly wronged. He was, indeed, not guilty of any crime. I therefore saved his precious life and I hid him."

"Stay! I command thee. If it really be as thou sayest and thou wilt show me Achikar alive, then will I give thee great wealth and make thy rank above that of all thy friends. Thou shalt not die, but thou shalt live as the king's friend in honor and happiness. Fetch Achikar quickly and my heart will rejoice."

Achikar came before the astonished king and all his courtiers.

After a brief interval Achikar came before the astonished king and all his courtiers. When Sennacherib saw
him he wept and was mightily ashamed to look him in
the face. He knew that he had wronged him. He cried
aloud: "Praise be to God Who hath brought thee back!"

Achikar turned to the King and said: "Because I have
seen thy face, my lord, no evil is in my heart."

"Hast thou heard of the letter which I have received
from Pharaoh, King of Egypt?"

"No, my lord King!"

"Read it, noble Achikar! Give me advice how to
answer it."

Achikar took it from the king's hand and read it. He
then said to the king: "My lord! concerning this matter
which Pharaoh demands, be not anxious. I will go to
Egypt and build thee a castle in the air. I will then bring
back with me the three years' tribute of Egypt."

When the King Sennacherib heard Achikar's words he rejoiced very heartily. Then Achikar said: "Grant me, I beseech thee, a delay of forty days. I need time to consider this matter so as to arrange it successfully."

The King most readily agreed to this. Achikar went to his home in the country and told his huntsmen to capture two young eagles for him. When this had been done, he ordered the workers in flax to weave two strong ropes, each to be two thousand cubits long and one ell in thickness. He also caused his carpenters to make two large cages for the eagles. He then took two little lads, making them sit every day on the backs of the eagles. The feet of the birds were bound by the long ropes to prevent them flying away. After a while the lads were quite accustomed to their morning ride on

Achikar ordered two little lads to sit on the backs of eagles.

the eagles. By means of the ropes the birds could be drawn down to the ground when necessary. Achikar also taught the boys to shout when high up in the air: "Bring bricks, bring clay, that we may build the king's castle up here, for we are sitting still doing nothing." After many days' training everything was in order just as Achikar desired. He went to the King's palace to tell him that he was ready to go to Pharaoh and to say "Farewell." Sennacherib embraced him and wished him a happy and prosperous journey. He then set out for Egypt, taking with him a company of soldiers, the eagles in their cages, the long ropes and the two boys.

At last he came to the land of Egypt. He went at once to visit Pharaoh in his palace. When he was brought before the king he bowed his face to the ground and said: "O my lord, O king! My master Sennacherib sends thee greetings of peace. He has read the letter written by thy Majesty and thanks thee mightily for the honor thou dost confer upon him by promising to give him three years' tribute if thy castle in the air is built. I have therefore come to Egypt, thy land, to build thee here a castle between the heavens and the earth. By the help of the Most High God and thy noble favor I will build it for thee as thou desirest. Please provide lime, stone, clay and workmen. I have brought with me from the land of Assyria skilled builders to complete thy castle."

The words of Achikar were heard by Pharaoh and his courtiers with great surprise. In fact, they could hardly believe their ears. The King gave orders to have all that Achikar demanded at once prepared and taken to that part of the desert where the royal soldiers were accustomed to drill. Thither came Achikar with his lads, the eagles and the ropes. The King and his courtiers also went there to see how the wonderful castle would be built.

Achikar let the eagles out of their cages. He tied the lads on their backs and also tied the ropes to the feet of the eagles and let them go in the air. They soared upwards, till they remained between heaven and earth. Then the boys began to shout, saying: "Bring bricks, bring clay, that we may build the King's castle in the air. We are sitting up here doing nothing."

The crowd watched as Achikar let the eagles out of their cages.

The crowd below around the King were mightily astonished at all that they saw. They wondered what it all meant and what was going to happen. Achikar took a rod in his hand and began to beat the King's workmen who were standing still with gaping mouths, surprised beyond measure at seeing the boys on the eagles high up in the air. He shouted for Pharaoh's soldiers, saying to them: "Bring up to my skilled workmen what they require, bricks and clay. Do not hinder them from their work."

Pharaoh turned to him and said: "Tell me thy name."

"I am Achikar, the secretary of State to the King of Assyria."

"Did I not certainly hear that thy lord and king had caused thee to be slain?"

"Be that as it may. I am yet alive, for God saved me to build thy castle in the air."

"Thou art indeed mad, Achikar. Who can bring up sand, bricks and clay to thy builders up there between heaven and earth?" said the King in a temper.

"How then, my lord King! shall we build a castle in the air? I have prepared all the plans and yonder in the air are the special builders. All they need is the material. I can also tell thee this—if my lord Sennacherib, the mighty King of the Assyrian Empire, were here, he would have built several castles in the air in a single day."

"Have done with the castle, Achikar. Get thee to thy King and I will send with thee three years' tribute. Would that I had never written my foolish letter to thy lord. Give him my greetings and tell him I shall never again ask for such an impossible thing as a castle in the air. We must learn to be satisfied with such things as are possible and right. Farewell, wise Achikar."

Straightway he returned to his lord, King Sennacherib. When the news reached the King of Assyria that the trusty Achikar was returning, he went out to meet him and rejoiced over him exceedingly. When they met, the King cried: "Welcome home, dear Achikar, the strength of my kingdom, the prince of my realm." Achikar told him how he had fared in Egypt, and with pride showed him the three years' tribute sent by

Pharaoh. King Sennacherib was delighted and said:
"Take of this tribute as much as thou dost desire."

"I desire naught but the safety of my lord the King. I
am happy to know that I have been able to serve thee.
Continue to trust me and I will do all I can to help thee
to increase in honor and greatness."

Achikar lived to be a very old man. To his last day
Sennacherib honored and loved him as the wisest man
in his kingdom.

The Snake's Thanks

THE FOLLOWING story was told at the court of David, King of Israel. It happened in those good times that an old man was walking along the road on a bitterly cold winter's day. He was feeble and had to support his old body upon a thick stick. On the side of the road he saw a snake, frozen with the cold. He felt very sorry to see one of God's creatures in pain. He went up to it and saw its eyes open and close. "Poor thing," said he, "it will soon die if it remain here much longer. Do we not read in God's Holy Bible that we must be merciful to all things which He has made? I will pick up the poor snake and try to revive it."

He hastened to take it up, and in order to give it a little warmth he put it under his coat close to his chest. It did not take very many minutes to warm it. The man was soon aware of the snake's recovery, for it began to coil its slimy body around him. Its pressure became gradually greater and greater till the man cried out in alarm: "Hold on! What art thou doing? Why dost thou squeeze me to death? Had it not been for my kindness and sympathy thou wouldst by now have perished on the roadside. When I picked thee up thou wast almost frozen to death. I have given thee back thy life and in return thou seekest to kill me. Is it right to return evil for good? Is this thy way of thanking those who help thee?"

"Thou art a very nice old man. But thou dost not seem to remember what I am. Tell me that first."

"Thou art a snake."

"Exactly. I am therefore quite in order in killing thee and any man. Snakes are made to kill the children of men."

"Come, Master Snake. Let us put our case before a judge and let us hear what he has to say."

"Very well, I agree to do this. Before whom shall we state our case?"

"Before the first creature that we meet on the road."

On and on they went till at last they saw an ox coming along. The old man was pleased and called out:

"Please, Master Ox, we wish thee to judge between us."

"Please, Master Ox, oblige this snake on my neck and me by standing here for a few minutes."

"What do ye want?"

"We wish thee to judge between us."

"What's the matter?"

"I found this snake perishing with cold. To save its life I put it on my chest under my coat."

"That was indeed most kind," said the ox.

"I then found that as soon as the snake revived it wanted to strangle me. Please decide whether that was right, and if not kindly order the snake to release its hold on me and to depart in peace."

"Now, Master Snake, what hast thou to say for thyself?"

"Yes, I admit that this good man speaks the truth. But I am quite right in trying to kill him."

"How so?"

"Because it is written in God's Book: 'I will put hatred between mankind and the serpent.'"

"Now," said the ox, "I have duly heard both sides. I find that the snake is in the right. It makes no difference that thou hast done it a good service and in return it kills thee. The world always returns evil for good. That is the way of life as far as I know it. Just see how I fare at the hands of my master. I work for him in his field from sunrise to sunset. At night I am shut up in a cold shed with a little hay and some oats for my food. My master sits in his cozy room with a lovely bright fire to warm him. He has a nice supper of fine fish and good meat. He even drinks sweet wine whereas I only get cold water. He sleeps in a clean soft bed whilst I have not even a coverlet over my back. In a year or two when I am no longer able to work in the field, he will sell me to the butcher who will kill me."

These words grieved the poor old man very much. "I am not satisfied with this judge," he cried aloud.

Leaving the ox behind he went on his way with the snake coiled around his neck.

"Let us try again, if it please thee," said the snake. "We will ask the next creature that we meet. I am sure I will win the case."

"Wait and see, Master Snake. Ah! here comes thy friend the ass. We will ask him to be the judge."

"By all means."

They both told their story in turn to the ass, just as they had told the ox. The ass also quoted the same words of the Bible as the ox. After a long tale of his own sorrows at the hands of ungrateful man, the ass decided that the snake was in the right.

"See!" cried the snake, "did I not say that I should win? I shall now kill thee and know that I am doing the right thing."

"Stay, Master Snake, let us be fair. We have asked two animals to judge between us. Let us also put the case before a man. It is natural that animals should judge in thy favor, for they are thy kinsmen. Come before David, King of Israel. He is a good man and will speak as is right."

"Very good, I agree."

When they came before the King, he listened very attentively to both of them. Turning to the old man, David said: "Why hast thou not kept the Holy Law? It tells us that God has put hatred between thee and the serpent. Thou hast forgotten this and now I fear I cannot help thee."

"Ah!" cried the snake in a spiteful voice, "I am in the right."

The poor man left the King's presence with a very sad heart, for the snake was beginning to squeeze him

*The old man told the lad how the snake
had entwined itself around him.*

more tightly than ever. He had now given up all hope.
He feared that the snake would kill him before nightfall.
On and on he wandered with a heavy step, leaning
heavily on his stick. At last he felt so wretched that he
sat down by the side of a well saying to himself, "I will
die here and the snake may fall into the well and get
drowned." He saw a handsome lad near by who came
running up to him and said: "Peace be unto thee."

"Peace be also unto thee, my son."

"What aileth thee, for thy face is as white as a sheet?"

"I am nigh unto death."

"Can I fetch thee a little water?"

"Nay, dear son, many thanks. I have just left King
David. Alas! he cannot save my life and I must die."

"Tell me thy trouble. Perhaps I can help thee."

The old man then told him all about the snake and
showed him how it had entwined itself around his neck.

"Just wait here for a few minutes and then I will go with thee to King David. Thy case shall be retried and justice will be done. I must just stay a little while here by the well. My stick fell into it and I told my attendants to dig up the ground yonder where the source of the well lies. This will cause the water in the well to increase. My stick, of course, floats on the surface. As soon as the water rises near the top of the well I can reach it and as soon as I get it we will go to the King."

This action of the lad seemed very clever in the eyes of the old man. He therefore resolved to return with him to the King. At last they came before David. The lad, who was Solomon, the King's son, fell on his face to the ground. His father told him to rise up. He did so and kissed the King's hand.

"May I speak, dear father?"

"Speak, my son."

"Why didst thou not decide this man's case in his favor?"

"Because it serves him right to find himself in his present unfortunate state."

"How so, father dear?"

"Because he did not act according to the teaching of the Holy Law."

"O father, give me, I beseech thee, permission to sit in judgment in this case."

"Most gladly will I do so, if thou wilt be able to prove to me that I have not done justice to this unlucky man. Come, beloved son, and sit on my chair of state. I will listen to thy words of wisdom. May the God of my fathers be with thee in judgment!"

Solomon sat on his father's chair and began to say to the snake: "Tell me, why dost thou do evil to one who has dealt kindly with thee?"

"God has commanded me to do so."

"Where?"

"In his Law."

"Dost thou agree to abide by the teaching of the Law?"

"Of course I do."

"Now at once get off this man and stand on the ground even as he does."

"Why should I?"

"Because the Holy Law demands that those who have a quarrel shall stand before the judge."

"I quite agree to do this. Now wilt thou judge between me and this man." The snake uncoiled its body and placed itself beside the old man. Solomon then turned to the old man and said: "The Holy Law has also a command for thee. It tells thee that thou shalt bruise the serpent's head. Do now according the word of thy God." The old man no sooner heard Solomon's words than he raised his stick on which he was leaning and smote the snake a deadly blow on its head. The next second it was dead. King David and his courtiers were mightily astonished at the wonderful wisdom of Solomon, whose fame soon spread throughout the land. The old man thanked the prince and the King for saving his life and went his way in peace.

The Goblin and the Princess

ABOUT SEVENTEEN hundred years ago there lived a very famous Rabbi named Simeon ben Yochai. His home was in Palestine. He spent all his time in teaching the word of God to the Jews who came to listen to him. In those days the Romans were the rulers of the Holy Land, for they had conquered the Jews. At that time the Roman Emperor disliked the Jewish religion because it taught its believers that there was only one God, the great Creator of all things. The Romans did not understand this simple belief. They had ever so many gods and goddesses, a god of the sea, a god of the sky, and so on. The Emperor even believed that he was also a god. All his subjects, except the Jews, prayed to his image. He thought that the only way to make the Jews worship him and the Roman gods would be to forbid them to keep their holy ceremonies. He therefore made a law telling the Jews that they must no longer keep their Sabbath as a holy day of rest. All the other Jewish laws were also forbidden to be kept by them.

When the Jews in the Holy Land heard of the Emperor's law they were deeply grieved. In their distress they cried to God for help. They also turned to their great teacher, Rabbi Simeon ben Yochai, and begged him to go to Rome to ask the Emperor to with-

draw his cruel and unjust law, so that they might worship God as their fathers had taught them to do. They
knew that God had so often worked miracles on behalf
of Rabbi Simeon. Had he not indeed deserved this
Divine mark of favor? Did he not spend day after day in
reading the Holy Word of God and in teaching its great
lessons? The good Rabbi consented to go to Rome if
one of the teachers, named Eleazar ben Jose, would be
his companion. The latter agreed to do as Rabbi
Simeon desired.

Without any delay they set out on their journey to
Rome. They prayed to God for His protection and bless-
ing. At last they reached the great city of Rome, when
Rabbi Simeon said to his companion: "Let us well consider what we have to do here. First of all we must see
the Emperor. Then we must try, with the help of God, to
persuade him to withdraw his harsh law. Let us face
our difficulties and overcome them. When we get to the
palace we may not be admitted. In that case we shall
not be able to do anything. Again, if we should be
brought before the Emperor, how do we know that he
will listen to us and consider our petition? Is it likely
that he will consent to cancel his own law? To do such
a thing is unheard of in mighty Rome. Well do we know
how the Romans rule the world. They rule according to
their own ideas and not according to the wishes of their
subjects."

"True, indeed," replied Eleazar, "are thy words.
Perhaps the good God will help us. Whenever Israel is
in distress He also grieves with them. Their sorrows are
also His. Come what may, we will present ourselves, if
God will, at noon to-morrow at Cæsar's palace. The rest
we will leave in the hands of our Heavenly Father. Now
let us look for the Jewish quarter of this great city and
find a lodging for the night."

They found what they required and sat down together to eat a very modest supper. They were alone. Suddenly they were startled to see in their room a little Goblin. It came near to Rabbi Simeon and said to him with a bow of its body: "Peace be with you, O masters of the Law. Ye know me not. My name is Ben Temalion.

Suddenly they were startled to see in their room a little Goblin.

You will probably not believe me when I tell you why I am here. The purpose of my visit is to help you. I know you have a most difficult task to perform. I think you know that this task is almost an impossible one. Is it not so?"

"It is as thou sayest," replied Simeon.

"Do you care to employ my services?"

"I do not like to make use of thy evil power."

"Stay, Master!" cried Eleazar. "Who knows whether the Heavenly Father has not sent this goblin to help us!" Turning to the Goblin, he cried:

"Speak, Ben Temalion."

"Command me, and I will try to obey."

"Tell us how thou art able to help us."

"I have all my plans fully prepared."

"What are thy plans?"

"I cannot tell you unless you both agree to let me be of service to you."

"We agree," they both exclaimed.

"Well, my plan is as follows. Know that the mighty Cæsar here in Rome has an only daughter, whom he loves more than his own life. She is, indeed, the most beautiful princess in the world. Her mother died when she was a little girl. Perhaps on account of this fact her father never refuses to fulfill her least wish. Now I intend this very night to go to the palace."

"What for?" they cried.

"I will tell you. I propose to enter her body. The princess will at once become mad. She will continue in this sad condition as long as I am in her body. When her father learns of her terrible misfortune he will do anything to have her restored to health. You two men must play the part of physicians. Go to the palace to-morrow at noon and demand to see the Cæsar."

"The guard may refuse to admit us."

"Not so. Say that you have heard that the lovely princess has suddenly become mad. This knowledge of a Court secret will impress the guard. You must then say that you undertake to cure the princess there and then. You will at once be admitted and taken to the presence of the Emperor."

"But I am not a physician," said Rabbi Simeon. "I have never heard that my friend here is skilled in the art of healing."

"That matters not."

"How can we cure the princess?"

"Listen, Rabbi Simeon. I will now give thee the power of healing her disordered mind. All that thou hast to do is to go to her and whisper in her ear my name, Ben Temalion. I will then leave her body, and moreover, I will give a sign that I have done so."

"What sign wilt thou give?"

"Of course the madness will disappear. But to convince you that I have really left the body of the princess, I will cause all the glass in the palace to break in pieces."

"Now, Ben Temalion, how shall we be able to see the princess?"

"When ye come before Cæsar to cure his daughter, he will cause the girl to be brought before you. She will call for thee, Rabbi Simeon."

"Why?"

"She will fall in love with thee at first sight."

"Mad indeed will she be to do such folly. I am an old man, nearly eighty years old. My white beard is enough to frighten any girl and to make her look elsewhere for love and admiration."

"Now remember all I have said. You must ask the Emperor to reward you for healing his child by granting a petition you will present to him when the princess has been restored to health."

"To be sure, that is the object of our mission. What reward dost thou ask, Ben Temalion, for thy service?"

"To help the children of men is reward enough for a goblin. Now let us wait till to-morrow and all will be well." The next instant the goblin vanished.

Next day the two Rabbis betook themselves to the Emperor's palace and demanded to be taken to the presence of the Cæsar.

"What is your business?" asked the guard at the palace gate.

"We know that the princess is dangerously ill. In fact she has lost her reason in the last twenty-four hours."

"How do you know this?"

"Never mind how. We *do* know it. Do not waste precious time. We have come to heal the princess. We are physicians staying overnight in this city. Now wilt thou lead us to the Emperor's presence?"

"Wait here, and I will have your message sent to my mighty lord, the Emperor."

After a brief delay the order came to admit the two strangers. When the Emperor saw the Rabbis he cried in a voice full of contempt: "How now! Do ye Jews dare to enter our palace and to come before our divine presence? Think ye that ye can work miracles better than the Roman physicians?"

"Tell us, mighty Cæsar, have the imperial physicians been able to cure the beautiful princess?"

"Thus far they have not been successful."

"We shall be successful even this very day. Know indeed that life and death are not in the hands of man, but only in the power of God in whom we believe. He has sent us, this is our belief, to heal the princess. Was not your Majesty's daughter so happy and well but yesterday? Was she not like a ray of warm sunshine on a cold winter's day? Did she not rejoice your heart with her bright and cheery smile?"

"Ye speak truly indeed. Come now, what do you demand as your reward if ye heal my beloved child?"

"Grant but one petition which we will put before your Majesty."

The princess stretched out her hands toward Rabbi Simeon.

"I swear by all the gods to do this. Know ye that the oath of a Roman Emperor is never broken."

"So let it be according to your imperial word," said Rabbi Simeon.

"Stay. Mark ye well, ye wise men of Israel, if ye fail to heal my daughter, ye shall be thrown this very day into the arena. The famished lions will enjoy their meal when they devour your bodies."

"We hear your Majesty's warning. Have no fear. We will heal the sweet princess. Now let us see Her Imperial Highness, if it pleases your Majesty; otherwise of course we cannot cure her."

"Let the princess be brought before us at once," cried the Emperor.

After a few minutes had passed, she was brought before her father and the Rabbis. She was deadly pale and seemed to be terribly frightened. Her eyes were staring at the two strangers. Then she stretched out her hands towards Rabbi Simeon and in an excited voice cried aloud: "Happy am I to see thee at last, O my beloved! Of thee did I dream last night. Come quickly and save me, for I am nigh unto death's door."

"Hush! my beloved child," said the distressed Emperor with deep emotion. "Come to me and take my hand."

"Go away, I know thee not, O stranger!"

"I am thy father."

"I say I know thee not. Never have I seen thee before."

"Speak not thus, dearest child."

"I want to go to my beloved yonder. He is mine and I am his."

Rabbi Simeon gave the Emperor a knowing wink and went close to the princess. He laid his hand very gently on her arm and whispered in her ear the magic name "Ben Temalion." The spell was broken. She was once again the smiling princess. Turning to the Emperor she cried in a happy voice: "O dearest Father, how glad I am to see thy face. I have had a most horrible nightmare. I have only just awoke. Who are these venerable old men? Where do they come from and why are they here?"

Before the Emperor could speak there was a terrific crash. Every piece of glass in the palace was smashed into atoms.

"What is that?" cried the Emperor in alarm.

The imperial servants ran hither and thither. They seemed to be dazed, fearing some fresh surprise. They came to the Emperor and said: "There is no one to be seen."

"Never mind," said the Emperor, "about the glass. It will be replaced. Now let us rejoice. My happiness in seeing my darling daughter restored to health knows no bounds." Turning to the princess he said: "These learned men have cured thee. I am now about to grant them any petition they may desire to make."

"Let us rejoice! My darling daughter's health has been restored!"

"I also," said the princess, "will give them precious jewels."

"Nay, gracious princess!" cried the Rabbis, "we will only accept thy noble father's favor. We ask for neither gold nor gems. We seek neither honor nor worldly goods."

"What do ye then require?"

"As your Majesty knows, we are Jews from the imperial province of Palestine. Your Majesty has recently issued a law prohibiting the observance of the Sabbath, Festivals and other sacred rites of the Jewish religion. We desire to serve our God in our own way. If we are true to God we will also be loyal to Cæsar, for it is God who raises up kings to rule the children of men. We teach our people to fear God and the King. We now put our petition before your Majesty; it is this—pray cancel the imperial law dealing with the Jewish observances."

"I have promised to grant your petition. Ye have done your part in restoring my dear daughter's health. I will at once do my share by ordering the law to which ye have referred to be canceled. Go back to your brethren in Palestine and tell them that as long as I live I will give them my favor and protection. Farewell."

With bowed heads the two Rabbis withdrew. Their hearts were full of gratitude to their Heavenly Father for His love and mercy.

David and the Insects

IT HAPPENED one day that David the son of Jesse was sitting in the lovely garden of his father's house in Bethlehem, not far from Jerusalem. He was resting after a long day's hard work. He loved to gaze at the beautiful flowers painted with the golden tints of the setting sun. Their sweet perfume also made his heart glad and he felt so happy to be alive in such a glorious world. Hark! The pretty birds were singing so grandly. They were surely praising God. He also would join in their songs of praise, thanking the great Creator for having made this perfect world with its countless beautiful things.

His happy thoughts were suddenly disturbed by seeing a large wasp attacking a spider. The latter had woven its web between two twigs of a rose-bush near by. At that moment one of Jesse's servants who was ofttimes mad came along with a large stick in his hand. As soon as he saw the wasp stinging the unfortunate spider he drove them away by striking at them with his stick. He then went his way, knocking off the heads of the little daisies and buttercups along his path.

"Well, I never," cried David in surprise, "thought that the world was as funny as I now see it is. I was delighted but a minute or two before with all the wonderful and beautiful things made by God. Now I find that in this lovely world there are also such useless creatures as I have just seen. What earthly use is there in a madman who knows not what he is doing, ever bent on destroying whatever he sees? O Lord of the Universe! Tell me, I beseech Thee, why hast Thou created wasps and spiders? The wasp eats honey and destroys the spiders. Of what use is it? It is not good for anything except to breed maggots. As for the spider, it spins all the year round and never garbs itself with its fine web it has woven."

The Holy One, blessed be He, answered saying:

"O David! Why dost thou despise the little creatures which I have made for the welfare of the world. An occasion will surely arise when thou wilt have great need of their wonderful help. Then indeed wilt thou know why they have been created by Me. Everything in My universe has its great purpose; even the madman whom thou mockest has also his part to play. Despise naught in the world. I love all things that are the work of My hand. I hate none of the things which I have made. I spare all things because they are Mine. To everything there is a time and a place. All My creatures praise Me."

David heard no more, for the Divine voice grew silent. There was a hush. The sun had set and the golden tints vanished. The cool wind of the twilight reminded David that it was time to get back to his father's flock and to secure the sheep for the night.

Years passed by. David was no longer the shepherd of Jesse's flock. He was now the champion of Israel. His wonderful victory over the giant Goliath made him the hero and favorite of the people. He was now the King's son-in-law, for he had married the daughter of King Saul. The princess was his reward for slaying the mighty giant. Unfortunately David's popularity brought him the envy of King Saul. At last the King sought to kill poor David. To save his life he was forced to escape and hide in the mountains. Saul and his men followed in pursuit. David was finally forced to take refuge in a small cave. "Alas!" he cried, "my enemy will now surely find me and slay me. Help me, O God! save my life."

A spider wove its web across the mouth of the cave.

The Holy One, blessed be He, heard his prayer and sent a spider to weave its web across the mouth of the cave. Later, when Saul and his followers came along, the latter saw the spider's web. They pointed it out to the King, who said: "Truly no man has entered this cave, for had he done so he would have rent the web. Let us not waste our precious time here, but rather let us hurry along the road where we may overtake our enemy."

When they had departed David came forth from the cave. He saw the little spider hanging to part of its broken web. He took it in his hand very gently and caressed it, saying to it: "Blessed is thy Creator and thou also art blessed." He then praised the Heavenly Father, exclaiming: "Lord of the Universe! Who can do according to Thy works and according to Thy mighty deeds? Verily all Thy works and deeds are wonderful."

David then continued his flight and went on his way until he came to the land of the Philistines. He thought that he would be quite safe there. At all events, Saul would leave him alone. Now the king of the Philistines, Achish by name, was a good and pious man. As soon as David's presence in his land was discovered, he ordered his servants to bring the Hebrew hero before him. He greeted him kindly and asked him why he had run the risk of venturing into the territory of the Philistines.

"I ventured to come here for I am not safe in the land of Israel."

"Thou art mad. Thou hast saved Israel. Had it not been for thee all thy people with King Saul would now be our slaves. Dost thou tell us that thy life is not safe in thine own land?"

"O lord King! It is even as I have spoken. I am persecuted by King Saul. He seeks my life and I am safer here than in the Holy Land."

"Why does Saul persecute thee?"

"Because I slew Goliath."

It happened that the brothers of Goliath were the body-guard of King Achish. They told the King that David was worthy of death for having slain their brother. Achish asked them:

"Did he not kill Goliath in a fair combat?"

"Have a care, your Majesty! David is entitled then to be the ruler of all the Philistines. Did not Goliath boast that if he slew the Hebrew champion the children of Israel were to be the slaves of the Philistines, and vice versa?"

David now saw that he was in a very dangerous position. It was almost certain that the brothers of Goliath would kill him if he remained in their land. How could he escape? All of a sudden the idea flashed through his mind that he might escape death if he pretended to be a madman. They might pity him and spare his life. He sat down on the steps of the palace and began to scribble in the dust. He also entirely changed his behavior. This strange conduct puzzled the Philistines.

Now King Achish happened to have a most beautiful daughter who was unfortunately mad. When he saw David's foolish pranks he said to his body-guard: "Why do ye mock me? Is it because my dear daughter is mad that ye think I like to see idiots? Is it for this reason that ye have brought before me this raving madman? Do I then lack lunatics in my kingdom? Send him back to his friend, King Saul. I have no need of such a hero."

The body-guard told David to go away. He went away with a merry heart. He thanked God that he had been fortunate enough to escape from the power of the brothers of Goliath. "Now I know," cried he, "that even a madman has a useful part to play in this most wonderful world."

When he came back to the Holy Land, King Saul gave him no rest. He was forced to live the wretched life of a fugitive. On one occasion God delivered his enemy into his hand. He chanced to enter a large cave where he found King Saul and his attendants asleep. At the entrance sat the giant Abner also fast asleep. David and

his followers had to be very careful how they entered.
Fortunately the legs of Abner were drawn up. David's
followers urged him to kill his enemy, now that he had
the chance. This he refused to do. "I will return good
for evil," cried he. To prove to the King that his life had
been spared, David cut off a piece of the King's robe

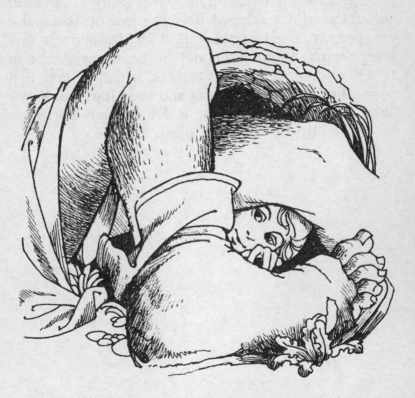

David was caught beneath Abner's huge legs.

and took hold of his cruse of water. David's men went
out and he followed. They had all left the cave except
David, who found himself caught beneath Abner's huge
legs. The giant had just stretched himself as David
wished to get out of the cave. "Dear me!" said David to
himself, "Abner's legs are like two massive pillars and I

am now caught between them as in a trap. O Lord! save me and answer me. My God, my God, why hast Thou forsaken me?"

The Lord heard his cry. At that moment the Holy One, blessed be He, worked a miracle by sending there and then a wasp to sting Abner. The pain caused the giant in his sleep to pull up his legs sharply. Thus David was released. He skipped over the feet of Abner and escaped. At once he praised God for His mercy in creating wasps. Never again did he have any doubt of God's wisdom in creating insects, which at first had seemed to him to be useless and even harmful. Never should we despise anything which seemed worthy to be created by the Holy One, blessed be He.

Joseph, the Sabbath Lover

IN ASCALON in the Holy Land there once lived a poor
peddler named Joseph. His greatest pleasure was to
keep the Sabbath Day holy. He was a good Jew, loving
God and man. The precepts of the Law were his delight
and by them did he live. He was not ashamed of his religion. In fact he was very proud of being a Jew. He had a
neighbor who was a heathen, very wealthy and selfish.
They often met and conversed with one another. This
was especially the case on Saturday when Joseph
abstained from his business. They would talk about
religion, especially about the Sabbath. Joseph would
dwell on the value of the Holy Day, pointing out that of
all the gifts bestowed by God upon humanity the most
precious was the weekly day of rest. Man is not a mere
machine, he needs rest and recreation. To those who
observe the Sabbath and call it a delight, its weekly
advent is like the arrival of a dear and intimate friend.

Joseph was wont to put by part of his daily earnings
in order to spend the Sabbath Day in a festive manner.
He often would stint himself and forego necessities on
weekdays so as to have better garments than his work-
ing clothes for the Sabbath and a fine spread of food on
his table in order to pay honor to the Sabbath. The
poor were always welcome guests at his table on Friday

nights and Saturdays. He not only honored the Sabbath, he also sanctified it. People called him "Mokir Shabbe," Sabbath Lover. He seemed to forget all his cares and troubles as soon as the Sabbath came. He never omitted to have a spotless white table cloth spread over his table. Then there was the Sabbath light burning in a beautiful silver lamp. Fresh bread and sweet wine were at hand for the Kiddush, or Sanctification. Meat and fish were abundantly provided. Joseph imagined himself to be a king and his fancy turned the Sabbath into a lovely princess, his bride. "Welcome! Queen Sabbath," he cried, "come, my beloved." What a delight it must have been to hear the Sabbath hymns sung at Joseph's table. He and his guests thanked their Heavenly Father for the Holy Day, the day of peace and repose. A gracious gift it was, leading the children of men to their Father in Heaven. It is a day for man whereby he can rise above material things and see something of the Divine vision.

One Sabbath Day the heathen neighbor, who was a miser, lacking nothing in the way of worldly material things, reproached the Jew for keeping his Sabbath. "How could any one," said he, "waste a valuable day by abstaining from work? No wonder you are poor. See, I am rich and possess more than I need. I am not only prosperous but I am also happy, for my motto is 'Live to-day and let to-morrow take care of itself.' You, and I suppose all the Jews are like you, think otherwise. You slave all the week for the sake of your Sabbath Day. I know you are kindhearted. Personally I don't believe in that sort of thing. I daresay you judge me to be callous and coldhearted, without any love for the poor. I certainly despise the poor, for it is generally their own fault if they do not get on in life. They are idle, foolish and careless."

"Good neighbor," replied Joseph, "I do not quite see the point of your lengthy remarks. You being by blaming me for keeping the Sabbath Day holy, and you then say that because I do this I am poor. You are rich because you do not keep the Sabbath. Now I admit that I am a poor man, but what of that? I am as happy to-day as a king. I have feasted well and I am resting. What more could I desire? You seem to think that the only pleasure in life is hoarding money. I differ and believe the best pleasures can be obtained when we spend money in a wise and good way. Perhaps you will always be rich and perhaps I shall always be poor, but if the question were asked: 'Who is the happier of the two?' I doubt whether you would be the one. Good-day, my friend! I must attend Synagogue for Sabbath prayer."

Joseph went his way trusting in God and loving to do His holy will, well knowing that the Sabbath was more precious than all the money in the world. "No man liveth by bread alone," thought he. Whilst Joseph was in the Synagogue his neighbor had fallen in with a brother heathen who was well known in Ascalon as a famous astrologer. They greeted one another and Joseph's neighbor asked him: "What dost thou read in the stars?"

"I read that thy fortune is on the wane."

"What dost thou mean?"

"Thy wealth will pass from thine hand to the hand of thy neighbor. This will happen within thirty days."

"Dost thou know why this must be?"

"Well do I know. The gods are very fickle in dealing with wealth. The poor man of to-day may be the rich man of the morrow. What use dost thou make of thy enormous fortune? I fear thou dost neither enjoy its benefits now nor wilt thou do so in the future. Tell me, who is thy neighbor?"

"Joseph the Sabbath lover, a Jew very poor and industrious."

"Of him have I heard. He will, so the stars seem to indicate, own all thy wealth."

"Here is a silver coin for thy evil prognostication. I fervently hope it will not come true. Now, farewell." They parted and went in opposite directions.

Fear took hold of the miser, and as he sat in his room that night staring at his gold and silver he cried: "Never shall the Jew Joseph have this money. I could not bear to see him rich and proud—and I should be poor. Horrible thought. It shall not be. I will defy fate and prevent my fortune going to the beggar Jew. He is a mean hypocrite; he deserves to be poor all the days of his life. I told him so this morning and now I am told that he is to have my money. This is ridiculous and far-fetched. The old Jew would say if he could read my thoughts: 'Man proposes but God disposes.' Well, I am going to propose and also dispose. Without delay I shall to-morrow sell all my property and buy precious pearls. I shall then leave Ascalon for good and settle in the fair lands of Italy."

Next day the miser converted all his wealth into a number of very beautiful pearls. He had them strung on a silken cord which he sewed on to his turban. That same day he left Ascalon and boarded a boat leaving the port for foreign parts. "I shall soon forget all about Joseph and the foolish astrologer," said he whilst walking on deck. At that moment a gale arose and his turban was lifted off his head and carried out to sea. At one fell blow all his fortune was gone forever. He cried and tore his hair out of his head, but all in vain. He was now a beggar.

Meanwhile Joseph was leading his usual life. On the next Friday he went, as was his wont, to purchase the

*A gale arose, and his turban was carried
out to sea with the string of pearls.*

best food for the Sabbath meals. He came to the fish-
market and saw a very large turbot on the dealer's
counter. Its price was very high and there was no one
who would buy it. As soon as Joseph saw it he gave the
full price without any discussion. In fact he felt very
happy, for he did not remember ever having seen such
a large fish. "It will not be wasted," he said to himself;
"the poor will help me to consume it." He thought that
it would be a sin to eat such a splendid fish on a week-
day, but for the Sabbath nothing was too good. He hur-
ried home in intense happiness and gave it with a
happy smile to his dear wife. "Here, my love, we have a
fish fit for a king," said he. "Yes, it shall be for a king, for
you, dear husband." He kissed his wife and went to his
bedroom to change his garments and to prepare himself for the Sabbath. He had barely reached the bedroom when he heard his wife's voice calling: "Come,
dear Joseph, come quickly."

He hastened to her side and asked her: "Why have you called me back?"

"Look, Joseph, see what I have found inside this turbot."

"It is a string of lovely pearls," he cried in delight.

"What a lucky fish!" she said.

He rubbed his eyes to make sure that he was not dreaming.

"See, my love! God has blessed us. He has given us wealth and we shall no longer slave during the six days of toil."

"Did you hear anything about our heathen neighbor with whom you were speaking on Sabbath last?"

"I heard that he had left Ascalon after having sold all his property here. I have also heard a rumor that he bought pearls with his money. How do we know whether these very pearls of our neighbor are not the same you have taken out of the fish?"

"It matters not, good Joseph, to whom they formerly belonged. It is quite evident that God in His love has sent this fortune to us. We shall know how to use His gifts even as we know how to love and appreciate His gift of the holy Sabbath."